AGENT ALINA

A Secret Agent inspiration for others
Agent Alina

Agent Alina

Soha Iman

Published by Soha Iman, 2024.

AGENT ALINA

First edition. August 30, 2024.

Copyright © 2024 Soha Iman.

ISBN: 979-8227239747

Written by Soha Iman.

Also by Soha Iman

Two Golden Heart's
Two Golden Heart's
Agent Alina
Journey Of An Artist

I Love To writing Books And Also Share My Ebooks To You All

Also by Soha Iman

Two Golden Heart's

Two Golden Heart's Agent Alina

Journey Of An Artist

Book Writer – Soha Iman
Category – Action, Adventure
Chapter – 1 To 9
About "
Hello I am Soha I like Writing Story Books I am 13 Years old

My Real Name Is Saniya Sultana You Like Reading Books I like Writing Books Have A great Journey ☺

1

Chapter 1

Chapter 1: The Beginning of a Dream

Alina was only 11 years old, but she knew exactly what she wanted to be when she grew up. While other kids in her class dreamed of becoming doctors or teachers, Alina had a different idea. She wanted to be a secret agent.

It all started one afternoon when Alina's father came home from work, tired but happy. He had been a soldier, fighting for their country and protecting its people. Alina admired her father more than anyone. He was brave, strong, and always knew how to make her feel safe.

One evening, as they sat together in their small living room, Alina asked him, "Dad, what does it feel like to protect the country?"

Her father smiled warmly and looked into her eyes. "It feels like doing something bigger than yourself," he said. "You work hard so that others can live in peace. It's not always easy, but it's worth it."

Alina nodded, hanging on to every word. She had heard stories from her father about his missions—how he had faced danger, traveled to different places, and worked with a team of loyal soldiers. Even though he didn't share all the details, Alina could tell that it was a tough job. But that only made her want it more.

"Can girls be secret agents?" Alina asked, her eyes wide with curiosity.

"Of course they can," her father said. "Being a secret agent isn't about whether you're a boy or a girl. It's about being smart, brave, and strong in your heart."

2

That night, Alina lay in bed, thinking about her father's words. She imagined herself sneaking through dark alleys, gathering important information, and protecting her country from harm. She could see herself stopping the bad guys and keeping her family safe. It was the first time she truly felt like she had a goal in life. She wanted to be an agent—someone who worked in the shadows, making sure that the people she loved were protected.

From that moment on, Alina began to change. She started reading every book she could find about spies and secret agents. Even though most of the books were fiction, she loved the idea of being able to outsmart the enemy. She loved how agents could blend in with the crowd, hiding in plain sight, and she practiced trying to be invisible in her own home.

Her father noticed her growing Interest and started teaching her small things. He would show her how to keep her body balanced, how to walk quietly, and even a few simple self-defense moves. Alina soaked it all in like a sponge, eager to learn everything.

One day, while they were out in the yard, her father said, "Being an agent isn't just about fighting or being sneaky. It's about knowing when to act and when to wait. Patience is just as important as skill."

Alina tried her best to understand. She wasn't always patient—she was only 11, after all—but she promised herself that she would work on it. She knew that if she wanted to become an agent, she had to be ready for anything.

At school, Alina was a quiet girl. She had a few friends, but she often kept to herself. While other kids played games during recess, Alina would sit by herself and observe. She watched the way people moved, the way they talked, and the way they interacted with each other. It was like she was practicing to be an agent already, even though she was still just a kid.

Her teachers often praised her for being focused and serious, but they didn't know about her secret dream. Alina didn't tell anyone about her plans. She knew that most people wouldn't understand, and she didn't want anyone to laugh at her. She kept her dream close to her heart, sharing it only with her father.

As time went on, Alina continued to work on her skills. She started running in the mornings to build her stamina, and she practiced solving puzzles to keep her mind sharp. She also studied hard in school, especially in subjects like science and math. She knew that agents had to be smart as well as strong.

One day, when Alina was sitting in class, her teacher handed out a writing assignment. "I want you all to write about what you want to be when you grow up," the teacher said.

Alina smiled to herself. She knew exactly what she would write about. But when she turned in her paper, her teacher looked surprised.

"A secret agent?" the teacher said, raising an eyebrow. "That's an interesting choice."

Alina nodded confidently. "I want to protect my country," she said. "Just like my father."

The teacher smiled warmly. "Well, if that's what you want to do, then I believe you can do it. Just remember, it takes a lot of hard work and dedication."

"I know," Alina said. "I'm ready."

As Alina got older, her dream only grew stronger. She started doing more research about what it took to become a secret agent. She learned that it wasn't an easy path—there were many tests and challenges along the way. But Alina wasn't afraid of hard work. In fact, she welcomed it. She knew that if she wanted to reach her goal, she had to be prepared to give it her all.

Her father continued to support her every step of the way. He encouraged her to stay focused and reminded her that becoming an agent wasn't something that would happen overnight. "It takes time," he would say. "But as long as you keep working at it, you'll get there."

Alina knew he was right, and she was willing to wait. She was willing to do whatever it took to make her dream come true.

As the years went by, Alina faced many challenges. There were times when she doubted herself, times when she wondered if she would ever be able to reach her goal. But every time she felt like giving up, she thought about her father and the lessons he had taught her. She remembered the pride In his voice when he talked about protecting their country, and she knew that she couldn't give up.

By the time Alina was a teenager, she was already more focused and determined than ever before. She had started training seriously, learning how to defend herself, how to stay calm under pressure, and how to think quickly in difficult situations. She was also working hard in school, making sure that she was as smart as she was strong.

But even as she trained and studied, Alina knew that there was still a long way to go. She wasn't an agent yet, but she was getting closer every day.

One night, as she sat with her father, she asked him, "Do you think I'll make it? Do you think I can become an agent?"

Her father looked at her with pride in his eyes. "I know you can," he said. "You have the heart of a true protector. And that's what being an agent is all about."

Alina smiled, feeling more determined than ever. She knew that she still had a lot of work to do, but she also knew that she wouldn't stop until she reached her goal.

And so, with her father's words in her heart and her dream guiding her every step, Alina continued her journey. She was still young, but she was on her way. One day, she would become the agent she had always dreamed of being. And when that day came, she would be ready to protect her country, just as her father had done before her.

Chapter 2: Trials of a Dream

By the time Alina was 15 years old, her dream of becoming a secret agent was no longer just a distant goal. It had become her life. She spent most of her time training, studying, and preparing for the day she would join the ranks of those who protected their country from unseen threats.

Her father continued to be her gre"test'supporter. Although he had retired from active duty, he still had a wealth of knowledge to share with her. Every evening after dinner, he would take her outside and teach her something new—whether it was how to defend herself in hand-to-hand combat, how to stay hidden in plain sight, or how to control her breathing to remain calm in high-stress situations.

Alina's mother, on the other hand, was more concerned about her daughter's obsession with becoming an agent. She worried that Alina was missing out on her childhood, that she was spending too much time focused on something that might never happen. "Alina, you're still so young," her mother would say. "Are you sure this is what you want?"

But Alina was certain. Every time she saw a news report about some terrible event happening in the world, her resolve only grew stronger. She wanted to be the one who made sure her country was safe. She wanted to be the one who stopped the bad guys before they could hurt innocent people.

Her mother would sigh, but she never stood In the way of Alina's dreams. Deep down, she knew that her daughter was serious, and that nothing could change her mind.

Alina's training became more intense as she grew older. She enrolled in martial arts classes, took up running to build her endurance, and spent hours at the library reading everything she could about espionage, intelligence gathering, and strategy. Her grades in school remained high, as she knew that becoming an agent required not just physical skill but mental sharpness as well.

But it wasn't easy. There were times when Alina felt overwhelmed, like she was trying to juggle too much at once. She was still just a teenager, and she sometimes longed for the simple pleasures her friends enjoyed—going to parties, hanging out at the mall, or just relaxing without a care in the world.

One afternoon, as Alina sat with her friend Hana in the school courtyard, Hana asked, "Why do you work so hard, Alina? Don't you ever get tired of it?"

Alina thought for a moment before answering. "I do get tired," she admitted. "But this is what I want more than anything. I can't stop now, even if it's hard."

Hana looked at her with a mix of admiration and concern. "You're going to be amazing one day," she said. "But don't forget to live a little while you're young."

Alina smiled, appreciating Hana's support. "I'll try," she said, though deep down, she knew that her path was different from most. She had chosen this life, and she was willing to make sacrifices to achieve her goal.

As the months passed, Alina's dedication only grew stronger. She began to research ways to join the intelligence services. She learned about the requirements, the entrance exams, and the rigorous training programs. She knew it wouldn't be easy, but she was ready for the challenge.

One evening, Alina sat with her father as they watched a documentary about spies during wartime. The stories of these men and women fascinated her—how they had risked their lives to gather information, how they had blended into enemy territories, and how they had made a difference through their courage and cunning.

"Do you think I could do that one day?" Alina asked her father, her eyes glued to the screen.

Her father smiled, proud of his daughter's determination. "I believe you can do anything you set your mind to," he said. "But remember, being an agent is not just about the thrill of the job. It's about serving your country and protecting those who can't

protect themselves. It's a heavy responsibility."

"I know," Alina said, her voice firm. "That's why I want to do it."

Alina's school offered an opportunity that seemed perfect for her. There was a summer program that focused on leadership, physical fitness, and problem-solving—qualities that would be important for anyone interested in a career in law enforcement or the military. Alina jumped at the chance to join, knowing it would help her prepare for her future.

The program was challenging. Every day, the participants woke up early for rigorous physical training, followed by lessons in teamwork, decision-making, and leadership. There were obstacle courses, strategy games, and even mock missions where they had to work together to solve problems under pressure.

Alina excelled in the program, but it wasn't without difficulty. The physical demands were intense, and there were times when her body felt like it couldn't go on. But every time she felt like giving up, she reminded herself why she was doing this. She wasn't just here to test her limits—she was here to prove to herself that she had what it took to become an agent.

One of the instructors, a former military officer named Captain Ryan, took notice of Alina's determination. "You've got potential," he told her after a particularly tough day of training. "But remember, it's not just about being strong. It's about being smart and staying focused."

"I know," Alina replied, wiping sweat from her brow. "I'm ready to work hard."

Captain Ryan nodded. "Good. You'll need that attitude if you want to make it in this line of work."

The program ended after six weeks, and Alina returned home feeling more confident than ever. She had learned valuable skills, both physical and mental, that she knew would serve her well in the future. More importantly, she had proven to herself that she could handle the challenges that came with pursuing her dream.

By the time Alina was 17, she had started to apply to universities. But unlike her classmates, who were focused on choosing schools with strong academic programs, Alina had one goal in mind: she wanted to attend a university that offered courses in criminal justice, international relations, and intelligence studies.

After much research and careful consideration, Alina applied to a top university known for its strong connections to the intelligence community. She wrote a passionate application essay, explaining her desire to serve her country and protect its citizens. She didn't sugarcoat the challenges she knew she would face, but she made it clear that she was ready for them.

When the acceptance letter arrived in the mail, Alina couldn't contain her excitement. She had been accepted into the program she had dreamed of for years. Her father hugged her tightly, beaming with pride, while her mother wiped away tears of both worry and joy.

"I'm so proud of you, Alina," her mother said. "But promise me you'll take care of yourself. This path you've chosen... it's not an easy one."

"I promise, Mom," Alina said, feeling a mix of excitement and nerves. "I'll be careful."

University life was different from anything Alina had experienced before. The classes were challenging, the expectations high, and the competition fierce. But Alina thrived in this environment. She threw herself into her studies, soaking up every bit of knowledge she could. She took courses in psychology, law, and international politics, all while continuing her physical training in her free time.

Alina also joined a student group focused on national security issues. They held debates, invited guest speakers, and even organized simulations of real-world crises. Alina loved every minute of it. She felt like she was finally on the right path, moving closer and closer to her goal.

But it wasn't all smooth sailing. There were moments when the pressure felt overwhelming. Balancing her studies with her physical training and extracurricular activities left Alina exhausted at times.

There were nights when she lay awake, doubting whether she could keep going. Was she really cut out for this life? Could she handle the demands of becoming a secret agent?

During one particularly difficult week, when the stress of exams and training had her on edge, Alina called her father. "Dad, I'm not sure I can do this," she said, her voice shaky. "It's just so

much. What if I'm not strong enough?"

Her father's voice was calm and steady on the other end of the line. "Alina, I know it's hard," he said. "But remember why you started this journey. You've always been strong enough. You just have to keep going, even when it feels impossible."

Alina took a deep breath and nodded, even though her father couldn't see her. "You're right," she said. "I won't give up."

By the time Alina graduated from university, she was more prepared than ever to pursue her dream of becoming a secret agent. She had the knowledge, the skills, and the determination. But she knew that the hardest part was still ahead of her. She would need to pass the entrance exams, undergo intense training, and prove herself in the field.

As she stood on the stage at her graduation ceremony, holding her diploma, Alina felt a sense of pride and accomplishment. She had come a long way since that day when she was 11 years old, sitting in her living room and dreaming of becoming an agent.

But this was only the beginning. The real journey was about to start.

Chapter 3: The Agent Emerges

Alina stood before the imposing doors of the secret intelligence agency's headquarters, her heart racing with both excitement and nerves. She had worked tirelessly for this moment, and now, at 27 years old, she was on the verge of achieving her dream. She had passed the grueling entrance exams, endured months of physical and mental challenges during training, and now she was ready to be officially welcomed into the agency as a secret agent.

As she walked through the halls, the weight of the years of effort pressed down on her. She had sacrificed so much to get here—her youth, her social life, and her time with friends and family. But Alina never doubted her decision. The thought of serving her country, protecting her people, and making a difference had driven her forward through every hardship.

When Alina reached the briefing room, she took a deep breath. Her training class had been whittled down to only a handful of recruits, all of them the best of the best. They had earned their place here, just as she had. Now, they were about to take the final step into the world they had only read about in books or seen in movies.

The room was quiet, filled with a sense of anticipation. Alina recognized a few of the faces—her fellow trainees, each of them showing the same determination she felt. At the front of the room, a senior officer, known only as Director Novak, stood waiting for them. He was a tall, imposing figure with sharp eyes that seemed to pierce through any façade. He had been with the agency for decades, and his reputation for demanding excellence was well-known.

When Director Novak spoke, his voice was calm but firm. "Congratulations," he said, his eyes scanning the room. "Each of you has proven that you have what it takes to join our ranks. But let me be clear—this is only the beginning. From this moment on, your lives will change forever. The work we do here is not for the faint of heart. It requires dedication, sacrifice, and an unwavering commitment to the safety of our nation."

Alina felt a surge of pride as the director's words washed over her. She had made it. She was about to become a secret agent.

The next few days were a blur of briefings, paperwork, and final preparations. Alina and her fellow recruits were given their first assignments—small missions designed to test their skills in the real world. These missions weren't life-threatening, but they were crucial in determining how well the new agents could operate under pressure.

Alina's first mission was a surveillance task. She was assigned to follow a person of interest suspected of leaking sensitive information to a foreign power. Her job was to observe, gather information, and report back without being noticed.

She spent hours preparing, studying the target's habits, learning the area she would be working in, and rehearsing her approach. When the day of the mission arrived, Alina felt a mix of nerves and excitement. This was her first real test in the field, and she was determined not to fail.

The mission went smoothly. Alina followed her target through the crowded streets of the city, blending in with the crowd, staying out of sight, and carefully documenting everything the target did. Her training had prepared her well—she was calm, focused, and never let her emotions cloud her judgment.

When she returned to the agency with her report, Director Novak reviewed her work. "Good job, Agent Alina," he said with a rare nod of approval. "You handled the mission well. But remember, this was only a small taste of what's to come. The real challenges are still ahead."

Alina nodded, grateful for the praise but fully aware that this was just the beginning. She knew that the missions would only get more difficult from here on out. But she was ready. She had been preparing for this moment for more than a decade, and she wasn't going to back down now.

As the months passed, Alina became more and more immersed in her new life as a secret agent. The missions grew more complex, the stakes higher. She worked long hours, sometimes spending days or even weeks in the field, gathering intelligence, tracking enemies, and working with a team of highly skilled agents.

But despite the challenges, Alina thrived in this environment. She had found her purpose, and every mission she completed successfully only strengthened her resolve. Her reputation within the agency began to grow—her colleagues admired her dedication and skill, and even Director Novak seemed impressed by her performance.

One of her most challenging missions came during her first year as an agent. A group of foreign operatives had infiltrated the country, and it was Alina's job to help track them down before they could carry out their plan. The mission required her to travel to a remote location, where she had to blend in with the local population while secretly gathering information.

It was during this mission that Alina truly realized the weight of her responsibility. The lives of innocent people were at stake, and it was up to her and her team to stop the threat before it was too late.

The mission was long and difficult. Alina spent weeks undercover, living in a small village and pretending to be an ordinary citizen. She had to be constantly alert, watching for any sign of the operatives while making sure not to blow her cover.

There were moments when Alina doubted herself—when the pressure of the mission seemed too much to bear. But she pushed through, reminding herself of the years of training she had undergone. She had been preparing for this moment her entire life.

In the end, the mission was a success. Alina and her team were able to track down the operatives and prevent the attack. It was a hard-fought victory, but it was worth it. When she returned to the agency, she felt a sense of pride and accomplishment that she had never felt before.

As Alina continued to prove herself in the field, she began to take on more leadership roles within the agency. She was no longer just a new recruit—she was becoming a seasoned agent, someone her colleagues could rely on in times of crisis.

But with her success came new challenges. The work was dangerous, and Alina had to make difficult decisions that weighed heavily on her. There were times when she had to choose between her mission and her personal values, and the consequences of those choices sometimes haunted her.

Despite the difficulties, Alina never wavered in her commitment to her country. She had known from the beginning that this job would require sacrifice, and she was willing to make those sacrifices if it meant keeping her people safe.

One of the hardest moments came during a mission where Alina's team was tasked with rescuing hostages from a terrorist group. The operation was risky, and there was no guarantee that everyone would make it out alive. Alina had to lead her team through a series of dangerous maneuvers, making split-second decisions that could mean the difference between life and death.

In the end, they were able to rescue the hostages, but not without loss. One of her teammates was injured in the process, and Alina felt the weight of that responsibility on her shoulders. She had always known that being a secret agent came with risks, but seeing the consequences firsthand was a sobering reminder of just how dangerous their work was.

By the end of her second year as an agent, Alina had established herself as one of the agency's top operatives. She had earned the respect of her colleagues and superiors, and she had become a trusted leader within the organization. But even as she achieved success in her career, Alina remained humble.

She never forgot the lessons her father had taught her when she was just a young girl dreaming of becoming an agent. She knew that her work was not about glory or recognition—it was about protecting the people she loved and serving her country to the best of her ability.

One evening, after a particularly difficult mission, Alina sat in her small apartment, reflecting on how far she had come. She thought back to the days when she was 11 years old, sitting with her father and dreaming of the day she would become a secret agent. Now, that dream had become her reality, and she was living the life she had always wanted.

But Alina knew that her journey was far from over. There would always be new challenges, new threats, and new missions to undertake. And as long as her country needed her, she would be there, ready to face whatever came her way.

As she looked out the window at the city below, Alina felt a deep sense of fulfillment. She had achieved her dream, but more importantly, she had found her purpose. She was an agent now—a protector, a defender, and a servant of her country. And she wouldn't have it any other way.

*Chapter 4: The Dark Shadows**

The clock struck midnight, and Alina sat in her dimly lit office at the agency, reviewing the details of her next mission. She had been an agent for nearly three years now, and though the thrill of her work still fueled her, she had learned that being a secret agent wasn't just about high-stakes missions and intense action. It was about patience, planning, and sometimes even doubt.

This next mission was unlike any she had taken before. It involved infiltrating a powerful criminal syndicate that had been operating under the radar for years. The group had connections to international arms dealers, corrupt officials, and underground networks that spread across several countries. Their influence was vast, and they had proven elusive to the agency for years.

Alina was chosen for this mission not just because of her skills but because of her ability to adapt. She was known for her calm under pressure, her intelligence, and her ability to blend in with any environment. But this mission would test her in ways she had never imagined.

The criminal syndicate was ruthless, and Infiltrating it would require Alina to go deep undercover for an extended period. She would have to assume a new identity, cut off contact with her usual life, and live among dangerous people who wouldn't hesitate to kill her if they suspected she was a spy.

Director Novak had personally briefed her on the mission. "This is going to be one of the hardest assignments you've ever faced," he had told her, his face serious. "You'll need to be someone else entirely for the duration of this mission. It's going to be dangerous, and there will be moments when you question everything. But I believe in you, Alina. You're the best person for this job."

Alina had nodded, accepting the weight of the task ahead of her. She knew this mission would be different from anything she had done before, but she was ready. Or at least, she thought she was.

A few weeks later, Alina stood in a rundown apartment in a city she had never lived in before. Her new identity was that of Maya Solis, a small-time criminal with a reputation for being cunning and resourceful. Her backstory had been meticulously crafted by the agency, complete with forged documents, fake criminal records, and connections to low-level criminals who could vouch for her.

Her mission was to slowly work her way Into the syndicate's inner circle, gaining their trust while gathering information that could lead to their downfall. It was a delicate balance—Alina had to play the part of Maya convincingly enough to fool the syndicate, but she also had to be constantly aware of her true purpose.

The first few weeks were a blur of Introductions, small jobs, and careful maneuvering. Alina kept her head down, observing everything around her. The syndicate was tightly knit, and they didn't trust outsiders easily. But Alina had been trained for this. She knew how to make people see her as one of them without drawing too much attention to herself.

One of the first people Alina met was Luka, a mid-level enforcer for the syndicate. He was rough around the edges, with a scar running down the side of his face and a permanent scowl that rarely softened. But despite his hardened exterior, Alina could tell that Luka wasn't as cold as he pretended to be.

Luka was the one who brought her into the fold, introducing her to others in the syndicate and vouching for her when questions were raised about her past. Over time, Alina and Luka developed a cautious friendship. They never talked about anything too personal, but there was a mutual respect between them that made working together easier.

Alina knew she couldn't afford to get too close to anyone in the syndicate. But Luka's trust was valuable, and she needed allies if she was going to succeed in her mission.

As the months passed, Alina slowly climbed the ranks within the syndicate. She took on riskier jobs, proving her loyalty to the group while secretly passing information back to the agency. It was a dangerous game, and there were times when Alina feared she was in too deep.

One night, after a particularly tense meeting with the syndicate's leadership, Alina found herself sitting alone in her apartment, staring at the worn-out furniture and the peeling wallpaper. She had been living as Maya Solis for so long that sometimes it was hard to remember who she really was. The line between her real identity and her cover was becoming increasingly blurred.

There were moments when Alina felt the weight of the deception pressing down on her. She missed her old life, the sense of purpose she had felt as an agent working openly for the agency. Now, every day was a test of her ability to lie, to manipulate, and to keep her true self hidden from the people she had infiltrated.

But Alina reminded herself why she was doing this. The syndicate was responsible for countless acts of violence and corruption. They had ruined lives, taken innocent people hostage, and trafficked in weapons that could cause untold destruction. Stopping them was worth the sacrifice she was making.

Still, the loneliness of her mission weighed on her. She had no one she could truly trust, no one to confide in. Even Luka, who had become something of a friend, was still part of the world she was trying to bring down.

Things took a turn for the worse when Alina discovered that the syndicate was planning a major operation—one that involved smuggling dangerous weapons into the country. The agency had been aware that the syndicate was involved in arms dealing, but this operation was on a much larger scale than anything they had seen before.

Alina knew she had to act fast. She began gathering as much information as she could, carefully documenting the syndicate's plans and passing it along to her handler at the agency. But the closer she got to the truth, the more dangerous her situation became.

The syndicate's leader, a man known only as "The Wolf," was a paranoid and ruthless figure. He trusted few people, and even those within his inner circle lived in constant fear of his wrath. Alina had managed to stay under his radar so far, but she knew that if The Wolf ever suspected she was an agent, her life would be forfeit.

One evening, as Alina was preparing to meet with her contact in the agency, she received an unexpected visit from Luka. He showed up at her apartment unannounced, his face unusually serious.

"We need to talk," Luka said as he stepped inside, closing the door behind him.

Alina felt a knot form in her stomach. She had always been careful around Luka, but something about his demeanor made her uneasy. She sat down, trying to remain calm as Luka took a seat across from her.

"There's been talk," Luka said, his voice low. "Some of the others are starting to get suspicious. They've noticed you've been asking a lot of questions."

Alina's heart raced, but she kept her expression neutral. "I'm just doing my job," she said, trying to sound casual. "I'm not looking for trouble."

Luka studied her for a moment before leaning in closer. "Listen, Maya... or whatever your real name is. I'm not stupid. I've been watching you."

Alina's blood ran cold. Had Luka figured her out? Was this the end of her mission?

Before she could respond, Luka continued, his voice softer now. "I don't know who you really are, and I don't care. But if you're planning something, you'd better be careful. The Wolf doesn't tolerate betrayal."

Alina looked at Luka, unsure of what to say. Was he warning her? Or was this some kind of test?

Luka stood up and moved toward the door. "Just be careful," he said again before leaving without another word.

The encounter with Luka left Alina shaken. She had always known that living undercover was dangerous, but now the reality of her situation was hitting her hard. If she made one wrong move, if The Wolf or anyone else in the syndicate found out who she really was, it would be over. There would be no second chances.

Alina doubled down on her efforts, becoming even more cautious in how she gathered and transmitted information to the agency. She couldn't afford to slip up now—not when she was so close to uncovering the full extent of the syndicate's plans.

As the operation drew closer, Alina knew she would have to take a more active role in bringing down the syndicate. She couldn't just pass information along anymore—she needed to act. But that meant putting herself directly in the line of fire.

Despite the danger, Alina was determined to see the mission through. She had spent years preparing for this moment, and she wasn't going to back down now. She had to stop The Wolf and his syndicate, no matter the cost.

But as the shadows around her grew darker, Alina knew that the price of success might be higher than she had ever imagined.

Chapter 5: The Unveiling of Alina's Secret Talent

The air was thick with tension as Alina sat alone in her apartment, staring at the faded cityscape outside her window. The mission had taken a dangerous turn, and every day felt like walking on the edge of a knife. Luka's cryptic warning still echoed in her mind, and she couldn't shake the feeling that she was being watched—closely. But now, more than ever, she knew she had to focus.

It was only a matter of time before the syndicate's grand operation went into motion, and Alina had to be prepared. But there was something else lurking beneath the surface, something Alina had kept hidden even from the agency itself: her mysterious talent.

From a young age, Alina had developed an ability that most people would consider impossible—a heightened sense of intuition that bordered on precognition. She had never told anyone about it, not even her father. It wasn't something she could control fully, but when she was under extreme stress or facing a dire situation, her mind would suddenly become sharp and clear. In those moments, she could see glimpses of events before they happened—flashes of insight that allowed her to anticipate dangers, avoid traps, and sometimes even influence the outcome of situations.

For years, Alina had buried this talent deep within her, relying on her training and skills to navigate the challenges of being a secret agent. But as the mission grew more treacherous, she realized that she could no longer afford to hide this part of herself. If she wanted to survive—if she wanted to take down The Wolf and his syndicate—she needed to embrace her gift.

A few days later, Alina found herself standing In the syndicate's headquarters, surrounded by cold, calculating criminals. The air was heavy with smoke, and the dim lighting cast long shadows across the room. The Wolf had called a meeting to finalize the details of the arms operation, and Alina had been invited to sit in on the discussion—a rare privilege, reserved only for those The Wolf trusted.

She sat quietly, listening as The Wolf laid out his plan. He was a tall, imposing figure with a commanding presence. His face was weathered and scarred from years of violence, and his eyes were cold and calculating. He spoke in a low, gravelly voice that demanded attention.

"The shipment will arrive in two days," The Wolf said, his eyes scanning the room. "We'll move it through the city and distribute it to our buyers before anyone even knows what's happening."

The plan was simple but deadly. The syndicate had smuggled in a large cache of weapons, and they were preparing to distribute them to various criminal groups throughout the country. The weapons would be used to fuel conflicts, destabilize governments, and cause chaos on an international scale.

As The Wolf continued to speak, Alina felt a familiar sensation stirring within her—an electric buzz in the back of her mind. Her senses heightened, and she could feel her intuition beginning to kick in. She closed her eyes for a brief moment, focusing on the energy coursing through her.

Suddenly, the room around her seemed to fade away, and Alina saw a series of flashes—quick, fragmented glimpses of the near future. She saw herself standing in a dark alley, facing a group of armed men. She saw The Wolf, his face twisted in anger, as he realized someone had betrayed him. She saw an explosion, fire engulfing a warehouse, and the sound of gunfire echoing in the distance.

Her mind snapped back to the present, and she opened her eyes. The room was just as it had been, with The Wolf still talking, unaware of the danger looming on the horizon. Alina took a deep breath, steadying herself. The visions were always disorienting, but they had never been wrong.

She knew now that something was going to happen—something that would put both her mission and her life at risk. But with her talent guiding her, she had a chance to stay one step ahead.

The day of the operation arrived, and Alina found herself standing in the very alley she had seen in her vision. She was dressed in her usual attire, blending into the shadows as she waited for the syndicate's convoy to pass through. The plan was simple—she would follow the convoy to its destination, gather as much information as possible, and signal the agency when the time was right.

But Alina couldn't shake the feeling that something was off. The vision had shown her a confrontation, and she knew that it was only a matter of time before things went wrong.

As the convoy approached, Alina's heart raced. She watched as the trucks rumbled down the narrow street, their cargo hidden under thick tarps. The men guarding the convoy were heavily armed, their faces set in grim determination.

Suddenly, a loud noise echoed through the alley—an explosion in the distance. Alina's breath caught in her throat. The vision was coming true.

Within seconds, chaos erupted. Gunfire rang out as a group of armed men ambushed the convoy. The syndicate's guards scrambled to return fire, but the ambush had been carefully planned. Alina ducked behind a stack of crates, her mind racing as she tried to figure out her next move.

Then, out of the corner of her eye, she saw Luka—his face pale and determined as he fought off the attackers. He hadn't been part of the vision, but now that he was here, Alina's mind began to race with possibilities.

Her intuition flared up again, and she knew what she had to do. She couldn't stay hidden any longer. If she didn't act now, the entire mission could be compromised.

Alina emerged from the shadows, moving with precision and speed. She slipped through the chaos, taking out one of the attackers with a quick, calculated strike. Her body moved on instinct, guided by the flashes of insight her mind provided. Every action was deliberate, every move calculated to avoid the bullets flying through the air.

Luka spotted her and shouted something, but Alina couldn't hear him over the gunfire. She gestured for him to follow her as she made her way toward the lead truck in the convoy. If she could secure the cargo, she could still salvage the mission.

But The Wolf was already there, standing next to the truck with a look of fury on his face. He had figured out what was happening—he knew someone had betrayed him. And now, his cold eyes were fixed on Alina.

"You," he snarled, his voice dripping with venom. "I knew there was something off about you."

Alina didn't flinch. She had seen this confrontation in her vision, and she knew exactly what to do. As The Wolf raised his gun, she moved faster than he could react. Her intuition guided her as she ducked under his aim, disarming him with a swift movement before he could fire a shot.

The Wolf stumbled back, rage and shock contorting his features. But before he could recover, Luka appeared at Alina's side, his own weapon trained on The Wolf.

"It's over," Luka said, his voice steady. "We've got you."

For a moment, The Wolf glared at them, his eyes burning with hatred. But then, realizing he had no way out, he lowered his hands in surrender.

Alina took a deep breath, feeling the tension in her body slowly start to fade. The mission wasn't over yet, but they had managed to stop The Wolf before he could carry out his plan.

Back at the agency, Alina was hailed as a hero. She had not only stopped a major arms operation but also taken down one of the most dangerous crime lords in the world. Director Novak personally congratulated her, acknowledging that her quick thinking and bravery had saved countless lives.

But what surprised Alina the most was Luka. After the mission, he had approached her with a serious expression on his face. "I don't know how you did it," he said quietly, "but you were always one step ahead. It was like you knew what was going to happen before it did."

Alina hesitated for a moment, unsure of how to respond. She had always kept her talent a secret, but now, after everything that had happened, she wondered if it was time to stop hiding.

"I have a way of seeing things," she said finally, her voice soft. "It's not something I can explain, but it's helped me survive."

Luka nodded, as if he had suspected as much. "Whatever it is, it saved our lives."

Alina smiled slightly, feeling a sense of relief wash over her. For the first time in a long while, she felt like she could embrace this part of herself—her mysterious talent that had always been both a gift and a burden. She didn't have to hide it anymore.

As she walked through the halls of the agency, Alina felt a renewed sense of purpose. She had faced the darkness, embraced her talent, and come out stronger on the other side. And now, with the syndicate defeated and her reputation solidified, she was ready for whatever challenges lay ahead.

*Chapter 6: A New Terror Unveiled**

Alina stood in the agency's briefing room, her sharp eyes fixed on the digital map projected on the screen. A red dot blinked ominously over a remote region, marking the location of an emerging threat. Director Novak had called this an urgent meeting, and Alina could feel the gravity of the situation as she glanced around at the other agents seated at the table. All eyes were on the map, but Alina couldn't shake the sense that something far more dangerous was looming in the shadows.

"This is no ordinary mission," Director Novak began, his voice steady but laced with tension. "A terrorist cell has been discovered operating deep within these mountains. They're highly organized, well-funded, and most importantly, they've acquired access to classified nuclear materials."

Alina's heart skipped a beat. Nuclear materials. The words carried a weight that no agent took lightly. The threat of a nuclear disaster was something every agency feared but rarely faced. And now, here it was—staring them down, with the fate of millions hanging in the balance.

"The terrorist group calls themselves 'The Ascendants,'" Novak continued. "Their leader is a man named Asim Rahil. He's former military, trained in advanced warfare tactics, and he has a deep network of loyal followers. We believe his goal is to detonate a nuclear device in a major city to send a message to the world."

Alina's gaze shifted from the map to Director Novak. She could feel the room tense up. This was the kind of mission that could break an agent. But Alina was no ordinary agent. She had been through fire and come out stronger each time.

Novak's eyes landed on Alina, and she knew what was coming. "Alina," he said, his tone serious, "this mission requires your unique skills. We need someone who can infiltrate Rahil's inner circle and stop this attack before it's too late. This is going to be one of the most dangerous missions you've ever faced, but I have no doubt that you're the right person for the job."

Alina nodded, her expression resolute. She had faced dangerous enemies before, but something about this mission felt different. There was a darkness to Rahil's plan that went beyond mere terrorism—it was an existential threat that could change the world forever.

"I'm ready," she said quietly, her voice firm. "When do I start?"

The journey to the terrorist cell's stronghold was long and perilous. Alina had been dropped into the mountains under the cover of night, her parachute allowing her to land silently in the snow-covered wilderness. The cold bit at her skin as she made her way through the rugged terrain, her movements careful and deliberate to avoid detection by Rahil's patrols.

Alina had been given a new identity for this mission. She was now known as Zoya Varga, a weapons expert with a criminal background who had spent time working with various underground arms dealers. Her cover story was airtight, with fake documents and a well-crafted history that would make it difficult for Rahil's people to question her loyalties.

As she approached the terrorist camp, she could feel her heart pounding in her chest. The camp was hidden deep within a valley, surrounded by thick forests and high cliffs. Guards patrolled the perimeter with automatic rifles slung over their shoulders, their eyes scanning the darkness for any sign of intruders.

Alina's intuition flared as she neared the camp. Her mind sharpened, and she could sense the dangers lurking ahead. She slowed her pace, using the trees and rocks for cover as she surveyed the camp from a distance. The cold air seemed to hang still in the night, and every sound felt amplified—the crunch of snow underfoot, the distant rustle of the wind through the trees.

Finally, she spotted what she was looking for—a weak spot in the camp's defenses. One of the guards had wandered too far from his post, leaving a small section of the perimeter exposed. Alina moved quickly, slipping through the gap and into the heart of the camp before anyone noticed her presence.

Inside the camp, the atmosphere was tense. The terrorists were on edge, and Alina could sense that something big was about to happen. She kept her head down, moving through the camp as if she belonged there, her eyes constantly scanning for any sign of Rahil or the nuclear materials.

After hours of careful observation, Alina finally spotted Rahil. He was standing near one of the camp's larger tents, surrounded by a group of his top lieutenants. He was tall and imposing, with a sharp, calculating gaze that seemed to take in everything around him. He moved with the confidence of a man who believed he was untouchable.

Alina's mission was clear: she needed to gain Rahil's trust, infiltrate his inner circle, and find out where the nuclear device was being kept. But getting close to Rahil wouldn't be easy. He was paranoid, constantly surrounded by armed guards, and he trusted no one outside his core group of followers.

Alina's mind raced as she tried to figure out her next move. She needed to make contact with someone in Rahil's inner circle—someone who could vouch for her and help her get closer to the leader. But time was running out, and every second she spent in the camp increased the risk of her being discovered.

The opportunity came sooner than she expected. Later that night, Alina was approached by one of Rahil's lieutenants, a man named Tariq. He was a wiry figure with sharp features and a nervous energy that made him seem out of place among the hardened terrorists.

Tariq had heard about Zoya Varga, the weapons expert who had supposedly worked with some of the most dangerous arms dealers in the world. He was intrigued by her reputation and eager to see if she could be of use to Rahil's operation.

Alina played her part perfectly, presenting herself as confident and capable but not too eager to gain Rahil's favor. She knew that in this world, desperation was a sign of weakness, and weakness was something Rahil had no tolerance for.

After a brief conversation, Tariq agreed to introduce her to Rahil the next day. It was the opening Alina had been waiting for, but she knew she had to tread carefully. Rahil was no fool, and any misstep could expose her as a spy.

The next morning, Alina found herself standing face-to-face with Asim Rahil. The air in the tent was thick with tension as he studied her, his cold eyes probing for any sign of deceit. Alina kept her expression neutral, her heart steady as she met his gaze. "I've heard good things about you," Rahil said finally, his voice low and measured. "Tariq tells me you have experience with weapons—especially the kind of weapons we need."

Alina nodded. "I've worked with some of the best arms dealers in the world," she replied. "If you need firepower, I can get it."

Rahil narrowed his eyes, clearly not convinced. "I don't trust easily," he said. "And I certainly don't trust outsiders. But if you prove yourself useful, perhaps we can do business."

Alina nodded again, keeping her answers short and to the point. She knew that gaining Rahil's trust would be a slow process, but she was willing to play the long game. She just needed to find out where the nuclear device was being kept before Rahil's operation could move forward.

As the meeting came to an end, Rahil motioned for Tariq to escort Alina out of the tent. But just as she was about to leave, Rahil's voice stopped her.

"One more thing," he said, his eyes narrowing slightly. "You wouldn't happen to know anything about spies, would you? The agency has been breathing down our necks for months now. I wouldn't want to discover that you're one of them."

Alina's heart skipped a beat, but she forced herself to remain calm. She turned back to Rahil and met his gaze head-on. "Spies?" she said with a slight smile. "I've spent my life avoiding them."

Rahil studied her for a moment longer before nodding. "Good. See that you keep it that way."

As Alina walked out of the tent, she knew she had just passed a critical test. But the real danger was only just beginning. Rahil was suspicious, and she would have to be even more careful from now on.

But Alina wasn't afraid. She had faced danger before, and she knew how to navigate the darkest of situations. With her mysterious talent guiding her, she was ready for whatever Rahil and his terrorist cell had in store.

Chapter 7: Uncovering Secrets

The days that followed were filled with tension as Alina worked to gain the trust of Asim Rahil and his inner circle. Her cover as Zoya Varga, the weapons expert, seemed to be holding up well. She was introduced to various members of Rahil's team and even given a few minor tasks to prove her capabilities. But Alina knew that the real challenge lay ahead—discovering the location of the nuclear device and thwarting Rahil's plans.

Her nights were spent In the cold, dark mountains, while her days were filled with careful maneuvering through the terrorist camp. The camp itself was a complex network of tents, storage areas, and makeshift buildings. Alina made mental notes of the layout, trying to piece together any clues that might lead her to the nuclear materials.

One evening, while Alina was examining the perimeter of one of the storage tents, she overheard a conversation between two of Rahil's lieutenants. They were discussing a shipment of supplies that was expected to arrive within the next few days. The way they spoke about it—almost with reverence—suggested that it was of significant importance.

Alina decided to investigate further. She approached Tariq, the lieutenant who had first introduced her to Rahil, under the pretense of discussing an upcoming weapons deal. Tariq seemed more relaxed around her now, perhaps seeing her as an ally rather than a threat.

"I heard about the shipment that's coming in," Alina said casually. "What's so special about it?"

Tariq's eyes flickered with curiosity but he quickly masked it. "You're asking a lot of questions," he said. "It's just some new equipment and supplies we need to keep our operation running smoothly."

Alina nodded, though she could sense that Tariq was holding back. "I understand. I just want to make sure I'm fully prepared."

Tariq's expression softened slightly. "I'll see what I can do about getting you more details. But you need to keep your head down. Rahil's been on edge lately, and he doesn't take kindly to those who pry too much."

Alina thanked him and left the conversation, her mind racing with possibilities. The shipment could be a crucial piece of the puzzle, and she needed to find out more.

The next day, Alina was assigned to help with the preparations for the shipment. She was given a position near the storage area where the new supplies would be unloaded. It was a risky move, but it was also a chance to gather valuable information.

As the day wore on, Alina observed the activity around the storage tent. Workers moved crates and barrels, and there was a heightened sense of urgency in the air. Alina's sharp eyes caught sight of several crates marked with international hazardous materials symbols. Her heart raced. Could these be connected to the nuclear device?

She carefully made her way to a more secluded part of the tent and used her skills to unlock a crate that had been hastily packed away. Inside, she found what appeared to be sophisticated equipment—items that could be used for assembling a nuclear device. The sight confirmed her fears: this shipment was indeed linked to Rahil's plans.

Just then, she heard footsteps approaching. Panicking, she quickly locked the crate and hid behind a stack of barrels. Two men entered the area, speaking in hushed tones.

"Everything's ready for tonight," one of them said. "Rahil wants the device in place before dawn."

The other man nodded. "We need to be extra careful. The last thing we want is for someone to find out about this."

Alina held her breath as they continued their conversation. From what she could gather, Rahil planned to move the nuclear device tonight. This was her chance to gather crucial information and stop the attack before it happened.

That night, Alina prepared for her most daring operation yet. She had managed to secure a basic layout of the camp's storage facilities, and she used her knowledge to navigate through the darkened grounds with ease. Her goal was to find out exactly where the nuclear device was being kept and to devise a plan to neutralize the threat.

As she approached the storage area where she had seen the hazardous equipment, she noticed increased security. Guards were posted at every entrance, and a series of locks and codes protected the inner sanctum. Alina knew she needed to be careful.

Using her skills, Alina picked the locks and bypassed the security systems with practiced precision. Inside, she found a heavily guarded room filled with high-tech equipment and crates. Her heart pounded as she spotted the device—its ominous, metallic form was unmistakable.

She moved closer, examining the device closely. It was a complex piece of machinery, its components intricately arranged. She had seen similar devices in her training but never one this advanced. She knew she had to act quickly.

As she prepared to disable the device, she heard footsteps approaching. Her heart raced as she hid behind a stack of crates, praying not to be discovered. The guards were making their rounds, and Alina had to wait until they passed.

Once the coast was clear, she returned to her task. She used her skills to carefully dismantle the device's triggering mechanism, ensuring it would not be able to detonate. It was a delicate process, but Alina's training and experience allowed her to work with steady hands.

Just as she finished, the alarms blared throughout the camp. The terrorists had discovered her presence. Alina knew she had to escape quickly.

In the chaos that followed, Alina made her way back to the perimeter of the camp, evading guards and avoiding detection. She managed to slip out through the gap she had used earlier and disappear into the mountains. Her heart pounded as she made her way to the extraction point.

Back at the agency, Alina briefed Director Novak and her team on what she had discovered. The nuclear device had been neutralized, and the immediate threat had been averted. But the operation was far from over. Rahil and his followers were still at large, and there were questions that needed answers.

Director Novak looked at Alina with a mixture of relief and concern. "You did well, Alina. But this isn't over. We need to track down Rahil and ensure that he and his network are dismantled completely."

Alina nodded. "Understood. I'll do whatever it takes."

With the threat temporarily neutralized, Alina knew that the real challenge lay ahead. The fight against terrorism was far from over, and she was ready to face whatever came next.

Chapter 8: The Final Confrontation (Revised)

Alina's successful neutralization of the nuclear device had given her and the agency a crucial advantage. However, the job was far from finished. Zane Parker and his network were still at large, and the agency needed to bring them to justice before they could plan their next attack.

Director Novak convened a meeting with Alina and her team to plan the next steps. The tension in the room was palpable. Everyone knew that the operation was reaching its critical phase, and any misstep could have serious consequences.

"Parker and his inner circle are still in the mountains," Novak began, pointing to a new map projected on the screen. "We've managed to track their movements and have a rough idea of their current location. But we need to move quickly. They're planning to disperse and vanish into the wilderness, making it nearly impossible to find them."

Alina studied the map closely. "What's the plan?"

"We need to strike fast and decisively," Novak said. "Our intelligence suggests they're holed up in a fortified bunker not far from their current location. If we can breach it and capture Parker, we can dismantle his network and prevent any further attacks."

Alina nodded. "I'll lead the operation. I know the terrain and can navigate the area without being detected."

The night before the operation, Alina reviewed her equipment and briefed her team. They would be using a combination of stealth and force to breach the bunker. Alina's role would be to infiltrate the bunker, locate Parker, and ensure his capture. The rest of the team would provide support and handle any external threats.

As the team prepared to move out, Alina felt a familiar mix of anticipation and focus. She had come a long way since her early days as a trainee. This mission was a culmination of years of hard work, and she was determined to see it through to the end.

The team moved out under the cover of darkness, making their way through the dense forest and rugged terrain. The air was cold, and the moonlight cast eerie shadows across the landscape. Every sound seemed amplified, and Alina's senses were on high alert.

When they reached the bunker, Alina and her team went over the final details of their plan. The bunker was heavily fortified, with armed guards stationed at various points. Alina's job was to find a way inside without raising alarm.

Using her skills, Alina and her team bypassed the outer defenses and made their way to the bunker's main entrance. The security was tight, but Alina had studied the layout of the bunker and knew where to find the access points.

They worked swiftly and silently, disabling the security systems and cutting through the outer layers of the bunker. Alina could feel the adrenaline coursing through her veins as they approached the inner sanctum.

Inside the bunker, the atmosphere was tense. Alina's team moved cautiously through the dimly lit corridors, their footsteps echoing softly against the concrete walls. They followed the map and Alina's knowledge of the bunker's layout to navigate their way to Parker's quarters.

As they neared the central chamber, Alina could hear the murmur of voices and the occasional clink of metal. Parker and his lieutenants were still present, discussing their plans and preparing for their next move.

Alina signaled her team to hold their position while she took the lead. She carefully approached the chamber and peered inside. Parker and his top lieutenants were gathered around a table, looking over documents and maps. Alina's heart raced as she spotted Parker—his imposing figure was unmistakable.

Taking a deep breath, Alina moved into position. She and her team were prepared for a quick and decisive action. Alina's plan was to confront Parker directly and capture him before he could react.

With a sudden burst of action, Alina and her team stormed into the chamber. The terrorists were caught off guard, their surprise evident as they scrambled to defend themselves.

"Freeze! This is a raid!" Alina shouted, her voice echoing through the chamber.

Parker's eyes widened in shock. He quickly tried to reach for a weapon, but Alina was faster. She moved with precision, subduing Parker and his lieutenants with a series of well-placed strikes.

The ensuing fight was intense but brief. Alina's team, welltrained and coordinated, managed to overpower the terrorists. Within minutes, Parker and his key associates were restrained and taken into custody.

As the operation came to an end, Alina stood in the central chamber, breathing heavily but relieved. The mission had been a success. Parker was in custody, and his network was dismantled. The immediate threat had been neutralized, and the world was safer as a result.

Back at the agency, Director Novak praised Alina and her team for their successful operation. "You did an outstanding job, Alina. Your skills and determination were instrumental in bringing
Parker and his network to justice."

Alina nodded, her expression a mix of satisfaction and fatigue. "Thank you, Director. I'm just glad we could prevent a disaster."

As she left the briefing room, Alina reflected on her journey. From her early days as a young trainee to becoming a successful secret agent, she had faced countless challenges and adversaries. But through it all, her dedication to her country and her unwavering resolve had guided her.

The world was still a dangerous place, but Alina was ready for whatever came next. With Parker and his network behind bars, she knew there would always be new threats to face and new missions to undertake. And she was prepared to meet them head-on. **Chapter 9: A Naughty Family Reunion**

After the intense mission that brought down Zane Parker and his terrorist network, Alina was granted some much-needed time off. Her achievements had made her a hero within the agency, but now it was time for her to reconnect with the people she cherished the most—her family.

Alina's family was a lively, mischievous bunch, always full of surprises. Her parents had always supported her ambitions, even though it meant she was often away for long periods. Her siblings, each with their unique personalities, had grown up considerably during her time away. They were eager to have their big sister back, even if it was just for a short while.

As Alina arrived at her family's home, she was greeted by the familiar sights and sounds of her childhood. The neighborhood had changed little since she left, and the warm, inviting atmosphere of her family home instantly made her feel at ease.

The front door burst open before she even reached It, and out rushed her younger brother, Bilal, with a wide grin on his face. He was now a teenager, taller and more mischievous than ever.

"Alina! Finally, you're home!" he shouted, pulling her into a tight hug. "I've got so much to tell you, but first—check this out!" Before she could respond, Bilal was already pulling a prank, squirting a harmless stream of water from a toy ring hidden in his hand.

Alina laughed, wiping her face. "Still up to your old tricks, huh?"

"Some things never change," Bilal replied with a cheeky grin.

Inside, the house was a hive of activity. Her younger sister, Samira, was busy in the kitchen, trying her best to help their mother prepare a feast to welcome Alina home. Despite her best intentions, Samira's clumsiness often turned cooking into a bit of a mess, and today was no exception.

"Oops!" Samira exclaimed as she knocked over a bowl of flour, sending a cloud of white dust into the air. She turned to see Alina standing in the doorway, covered in flour but smiling.

"Looks like you've been busy," Alina said, her voice filled with amusement.

Samira blushed, but before she could apologize, their mother, Amina, stepped in, chuckling softly. "Welcome home, Alina. We've missed you so much."

"I've missed you too, Mom," Alina said, embracing her mother.

The evening was filled with laughter, stories, and delicious food. Alina's father, Jamal, who was always the more serious and disciplined one in the family, couldn't hide his pride as he listened to Alina's tales of her latest mission, though he kept reminding everyone that it was best to focus on family now.

"Your work is important, Alina, but it's good to have you home where you can relax," Jamal said as he poured tea for everyone. "You've done your duty. Now, let's enjoy this time together."

As the evening wore on, the conversation turned to the antics of Bilal, Samira, and their youngest sibling, Nadia, who had grown into a quiet, thoughtful girl with a knack for getting into innocent trouble without even trying.

"Do you remember the time Bilal tried to build a rocket in the backyard?" Samira asked, giggling.

"Oh, don't remind me," Alina said, shaking her head with a smile. "That was a disaster waiting to happen."

"But it would have worked if you hadn't stopped me!" Bilal protested, clearly still proud of his long-abandoned project.

"And saved the backyard from becoming a crater," Alina retorted, ruffling his hair.

Nadia, who had been listening quietly, suddenly spoke up. "Alina, are you going to leave again soon?"

The room fell silent as everyone looked at Alina. She smiled gently at Nadia and reached out to hold her hand. "Not for a while, Nadia. I'm going to stay here with all of you for some time. We'll have plenty of time to play, and I'll even help you with your school projects."

Nadia's face lit up with joy. "Promise?"

"Promise," Alina replied, sealing it with a pinky swear.

Over the next few days, Alina fully embraced the joy of being with her family. Despite the occasional prank from Bilal, the clumsiness of Samira, and Nadia's endless questions, she felt a deep sense of peace that she hadn't experienced in years. The bond with her family was stronger than ever, and she cherished every moment.

One day, as Alina and her siblings sat together in the living room, Bilal suddenly jumped up, his eyes gleaming with mischief. "Alina, I've got an idea! Let's play a game—'The Secret Agent Challenge'!"

Samira groaned playfully. "Not this again. Last time, you almost broke the TV."

But Bilal was undeterred. "Come on, it'll be fun! Alina's the real secret agent, so she can be the referee."

Nadia clapped her hands in excitement. "Yes! Let's do it!"

Alina laughed, knowing there was no way out of this. "Alright, but let's keep it safe this time, okay?"

The "Secret Agent Challenge" was a game Bilal had invented where they would set up obstacle courses and pretend to be spies on a mission. It was a mix of hide-and-seek, tag, and a lot of imaginative storytelling. Despite her years of real-life training and missions, Alina found herself enjoying the game just as much as her siblings.

As they crawled under tables, jumped over cushions, and "disarmed" imaginary traps, the house echoed with laughter. Even Jamal, usually serious, couldn't help but chuckle as he watched his children and wife join in the fun.

Later that evening, as the family sat together, exhausted from the day's activities, Alina felt a deep contentment. She knew she would eventually have to return to her duties, but for now, she was happy to be here, surrounded by the people she loved most.

Jamal, noticing the thoughtful look on Alina's face, spoke gently. "Alina, you've made us proud with everything you've accomplished. But remember, it's okay to take time for yourself.

Family is just as important as any mission."

Alina nodded, her heart full. "I know, Dad. And I'm going to make sure I'm here for all of you, just as much as I'm there for the agency."

Amina smiled warmly. "That's all we've ever wanted, Alina. To have you safe and happy, with us."

As the night drew on, the family settled into a comfortable silence, the warmth of their bond wrapping around them like a blanket. Alina knew that no matter where her work took her, she would always have a home to return to—a place where she was loved for who she was, not just for what she did.

And so, Alina's story came full circle. From a young girl with dreams of becoming a secret agent to a woman who had accomplished those dreams and more, she had learned that true success was not just in her achievements, but in the love and happiness she shared with her family.

No matter what challenges the future held, Alina knew she would face them with the strength and support of her family by her side. Together, they would continue to write the story of their lives, full of love, laughter, and perhaps a few more pranks along the way.

Hello SIReaders I Hope You Liked The Story What should we learn from this story

The story of Alina teaches several important lessons:

1. **Dedication and Perseverance**: Alina's journey fromchildhood to becoming a secret agent highlights the value of dedication and perseverance. She faced many challenges but remained committed to her dream, showing that hard work and determination can lead to success.
2. **Love for One's Country**: Alina's deep love for hercountry drives her actions throughout the story. Her sense of duty and patriotism reminds us of the importance of serving a cause greater than ourselves.
3. **The Importance of Family**: Despite her intense career,Alina never loses sight of the importance of her family. The story emphasizes that no matter how successful one becomes, the love and support of family are invaluable.

They provide a sense of belonging and balance in life.

4. **Balancing Work and Personal Life**: Alina's return toher family after completing her mission shows the need to balance work with personal life. Success is not just about professional achievements but also about finding happiness and fulfillment in personal relationships.

5. **Humility and Compassion**: Alina remains humble andcompassionate throughout her journey. She doesn't let her success change who she is at her core, maintaining strong, loving connections with those around her.

In essence, the story teaches that true success is a combination of professional achievements and the meaningful relationships we nurture with loved ones. It's about finding balance, staying grounded, and appreciating the simple joys of life.

Don't miss out!

Visit the website below and you can sign up to receive emails whenever Soha Iman publishes a new book. There's no charge and no obligation.

https://books2read.com/r/B-A-AFSCC-YEJXE

BOOKS 2 READ

Connecting independent readers to independent writers.

About the Publisher

Don't miss out!

Visit the website below and you can sign up to receive emails whenever Soha Iman publishes a new book. There's no charge and no obligation.

https://books2read.com/r/B-A-AFSCC-YEJXE

BOOKS 2 READ

Connecting independent readers to independent writers.

About the Author

Author - Soha Iman

www.ingramcontent.com/pod-product-compliance
Lightning Source LLC
Chambersburg PA
CBHW021323160726

47994CB00004B/1580